Professor
Kompressor

PROFESSOR KOMPRESSOR

ISBN: 148397751X
ISBN-13: 978-1483977515

For Elizabeth

CONTENTS

DISCLAIMER

This is a work of fiction. All characters and incidents are the product of the author's imagination. Any resemblance with reality is entirely coincidental. Modern science and technology have led to many concepts that stretch our imagination, but they are not quite at the level described in this work.

CHAPTER 1

The Professor

Professor Kompressor lived in an attractive old house just outside a small countryside village. He was a clever man that had spent many years at school, learning all sorts of things. His head was always brimming with ideas. Many of them seemed sensational and simply wonderful. That was why people called him Professor. His real name was Aloysius, but nobody ever called him that. In fact, very few people knew. To everyone in the village he was simply known as the Professor.

Professor Kompressor was an inventor. He was excellent at inventing, but his inventions were not always excellent. Actually, they rarely worked as planned. Sometimes they did not work at all.

The Professor's house was far too large for him to care for, especially since he was pretty much always busy thinking about stuff, making things up or trying to piece together some fanciful piece of machinery or other. As a result, the house was a complete mess. Luckily, the Professor had a very understanding housekeeper. Her name was Maud, and she visited once or twice a week to make sure that the Professor was alright and the house was still standing where it was supposed to.

At the back of the house there was an enormous room. It may originally have been a ballroom, but now it was Professor Kompressor's inventing studio. It was jam packed full of useful inventing. Everything from small electronic parts to pieces of heavy machinery covered every available surface. In the middle of the room stood a small desk. This was where the Professor put his inventions together. Next to the desk was a frayed old chair. This was where the Professor sat when he was inventing. He never noticed that the chair was falling apart. He was too busy thinking about his inventions.

The house had many other rooms, but most of them were rarely used. Upstairs was a small bedroom where Professor Kompressor slept when he actually remembered to go to bed. Downstairs was the kitchen, which was surprisingly tidy compared to the rest of the house. Even though the Professor was not particularly interested in cooking, he knew how to make beans on toast and a few other dishes. Sausages, bacon and eggs, meatballs, chips... He may not have kept the best of diets, but at least he managed to keep himself going.

The most important appliance in the kitchen was the kettle. Professor Kompressor simply would not have survived without the kettle. He needed it to boil water to make tea. And he absolutely needed tea to get by. And invent. A nice mug of tea with three lumps of sugar and a splash of milk, just the thing to keep a busy brain going.

Professor Kompressor also needed a comfortable place to sit to enjoy his tea, and to think, of course. Sometimes he sat on an old chair in the overgrown garden, which was more like a jungle with plants sprouting all over the place and grass that always needed cutting. The Professor enjoyed sitting outside in the fresh air listening to the birds twittering in the shrubbery, but more often than not he stayed inside. His favourite place, apart from the inventing studio, was the sitting room. In the sitting room he had an old flower patterned chair, which was extremely comfortable. It was so extremely comfortable because Professor Kompressor had sat in it so often that it had shaped itself after his body. The chair would have been extremely uncomfortable to anyone else, but it was perfect for the Professor.

In the sitting room there was an old radio, which the Professor listened to whenever he felt the need to find out what was going on in the world. There was also a small television...

CHAPTER 2

The Telepathic Television

Professor Kompressor was a busy man.

In between inventing and sleeping there was not much time left for anything else, but every now and then he needed a break.

To give his busy brain a rest he liked to read books, do crossword puzzles, listen to the news on the radio and occasionally watch something entertaining on television.

The big problem with the television was that there was never anything on that he wanted to watch. At least not when he wanted to watch it.

"The problem with the television is that one can never find anything worth watching," thought the Professor.

"Someone ought to invent a better television that only shows programmes that you want to see, when you want to see them."

"Yes," he decided. "Someone really ought to do that."

He sat back in his comfortable chair, took a sip of tea, three lumps of sugar and a splash of milk, and thought for a while.

Then it struck him.

"... but I am an inventor!" he said out loud. "I am excellent at inventing. I will invent a better television. That's what I'll do."

After a fitful night's sleep, when he had not been able to stop his brain from thinking, he got up and down to business.

"The real problem with the television is that you can't find what you want among the many different channels," he thought. "It's simply too confusing."

"What you need is a way to make the machine show what you want to see, whenever you want to see it."

"That's just what you need," he concluded, "but how do I build such a thing?"

Professor Kompressor worked hard all morning, but made very little progress on his invention. By lunchtime he was tired, hungry and in need of a break.

He went into the kitchen to make a fresh pot of tea and some cheese sandwiches, which he brought into the sitting room on a small tray. He switched on the radio, and sat down in his comfortable chair to enjoy his snack.

The chair was a little bit too comfortable and the Professor was a little bit too tired.

"No harm in a little snooze," he thought, and then he was asleep.

As he was sleeping, the radio droned on. It was tuned to a programme discussing the human brain, and occasional words and phrases seemed to float in the air, entering the Professor's dreams.

"... telekinesis, the ability to move things around by thinking about them..."

"... the mysteries of the brain..."

"... its vast, untapped potential..."

"... thought control..."

The Professor woke up with a start.

"I've got it!" he shouted. "Thought control! That's the thing!"

"You need to be able control the television with your mind. That would be the ultimate remote control."

"I simply need to build a television that shows exactly the kind of programme you think about, the moment you think about it."

"A telepathic television!"

"... but how do I do that?"

With renewed vigour, the Professor went back to the inventing studio to sketch the plans for the new device. Then he started putting it together. This was not easy, but the Professor was clever. It took all afternoon and most of the evening, but finally he was done. When he put down his tools it was dark outside. He stood up, yawned and decided it would be best to test the invention in the morning.

That night he slept like a baby, pleased with the day's work.

The next morning, after the cup of tea he needed to get going, the Professor brought the telepathic television into the sitting room. He put it on a small table and sat down in his comfortable chair. He was very excited.

He switched on the television. The picture flickered, as if it did not quite know what channel was supposed to be on. The Professor felt his excitement turn to frustration.

"It doesn't work," he thought. "After all that effort."

The television finally settled on a channel. A woman was crying, makeup running in little streams down her cheeks. There was sad music in the background.

"What's this?" thought the Professor. "I don't want to watch this!"

"Sentimental drivel," he grumbled.

He was getting frustrated and just a bit angry.

The television flickered and the channel changed to what looked like an old western movie. Two cowboys were fighting in a saloon. Crash, bang, pow! Furniture was being smashed to pieces all over the place. Quite chaotic.

"No," complained the Professor, who could not make any sense of it. "Don't like this either!"

"Why does the infernal machine not show something I actually want to see?"

"I need a cup of tea to calm me down," he thought.

Again, the television flickered and the

channel changed. This time to a commercial. The famous actress Leia Skymap was sitting on a sofa sipping from a cup. She was saying something about the essentials of tea in her deep, husky voice.

The Professor did not see this because he was already in the kitchen, filling up the kettle.

When he returned to the sitting room he was both frustrated and confused.

There was a cartoon on the television. Some weird looking creatures were fighting one another in what seemed to be some sort of duel. An explosion of colours and loud sound effects.

"What on earth is this?" thought the Professor. "I certainly don't want to watch this. No fun at all."

He took a mouthful of tea.

The television switched channel. Another well-known actress was sitting on a comfortable chair, steaming cup in hand, advertising a relaxing night time drink.

"Must be a commercial break," thought the Professor. "Just what I wanted to avoid."

"This invention simply doesn't work."

Then it struck him.

The invention did work. In fact, it worked a little bit too well. The channels changed as the Professor's mind wandered. It might have seemed like a good idea, but in reality it was just not very practical.

Disappointed, the Professor put the telepathic television away in the garden shed and never thought about it again.

CHAPTER 3

The Mechanical Maid

Professor Kompressor's house was a complete mess. It did not matter that Maud, the once-or-twice-a-week housekeeper, did her best to tidy up. The Professor was simply too good at picking things up, moving them about and leaving them where they were not supposed to be. When Maud complained, the Professor muttered something about the "laws of thermodynamics" and that "disorder must increase". This sounded like complete gobbledygook, so Maud ignored the Professor and quietly carried on cleaning. She knew perfectly well that it was possible to keep a home nice and tidy. There was absolutely no reason why chaos should be allowed to reign.

The Professor did not usually notice the mess that he lived in. But there were times when he could not find something he was looking for. He knew just where he had put it, but it was not there to be found. Instead he kept finding things he was not looking for, all in the wrong place.

This was one of those times.

"That infernal woman," he thought to himself, quite unfairly blaming Maud.

"She's always moving things about, leaving them where they're not supposed to be."

"... and she's always complaining that the house is a mess."

"I need to do something about this," he thought, "but what?"

Then came the day when Maud had to go to look after her sick aunt in the village of Diawn Diolch on the Welsh borders. She could not say how long she would be away. The Professor realized that he needed someone to help out around the house, but he could not afford to pay for it.

"Maybe I could invent something?" he thought.

"Yes, that's the answer!"

"I'll invent a mechanical helper. A mechanical maid, programmed for housework and cooking, that never sleeps or needs a rest."

"That's what I need."

However, it was too late to do any inventing that day, so the Professor decided to go to bed. He would start on the invention the next day.

Getting out of bed the following morning, the first thing the Professor thought about was a nice cup of tea. Three lumps of sugar and a splash of milk, as usual. Then he turned his mind to the mechanical maid. How would he construct such a thing?

After pondering the problem over breakfast, the Professor came to the conclusion that what he needed was a human-like robot that responded to simple commands like "Make some fresh tea. You know how I like it," or "Please tidy up the sitting room." Maybe even, "Why don't you do the dishes?"

It would be nice if the maid could talk, so that it could ask for new instructions after finishing a task. A talking maid would provide a bit of company, as well, whenever the Professor felt lonely.

Having made his plan, Professor

Kompressor spent the rest of the day in the inventing studio. He made numerous drawings of the mechanical maid, both of the design itself and the electronics that needed to go into it to make it work. He also spent time trying to find recordings of his favourite actress, Leia Skymap, whose beautiful voice would be perfect for the mechanical maid.

It was a very pleased Professor that went to bed that evening. He had managed to solve the tricky problems associated with the invention and now all he had to do was find the parts and put them together. This should not be very difficult.

It did not seem quite so easy in the morning, however. The Professor had to work hard, but by teatime he was done. The slim metallic maid, gleaming in the light of the workbench lamp, was ready to be switched on. Understandably excited, the Professor flicked the on-off switch. With a slight whirr, the electronic circuitry warmed up. A soft blue light came on in the maid's eyes, and there was a twitch in the arms and legs.

"Good evening, Professor," said the maid

in Leia Skymap's husky voice. "What can I do for you? Your wish is my command."

"It works!" thought the Professor.

"Brilliant!"

He considered for a moment and then made his request.

"Please go to the kitchen and make me a nice cup of tea."

"Yes, Professor," said the maid and rolled off towards the kitchen on its little wheels.

A couple of minutes passed. The Professor felt both nervous and excited. When the maid came back from the kitchen it was carrying a steaming cup. Very promising. The maid handed the Professor the cup and he took a sip.

"Eurgh!" he gasped. "Disgusting!"

"What kind of concoction is this? It's most certainly not tea."

"It is tea, Professor," said the maid calmly.

The Professor knew perfectly well that it was not tea. He strongly suspected that it was coffee with a splash of washing-up liquid, but he could not see the point of arguing with a machine.

He decided to test the maid in a different way.

"Please tidy up the sitting room," he said.

"Yes, Professor," said the maid, leaving the inventing studio on whirring wheels.

The Professor waited for a while. Then he sneaked into the hallway to peak through the door to see what the maid was up to. What he saw was most astonishing. The maid was standing in the middle of the room, absolutely still.

Doing nothing whatsoever.

"My goodness," thought the Professor. "What's going on?"

Then he realized what the problem was. The maid did not have the faintest clue what to do. It had only been programmed to follow very basic instructions. It had the ability to learn, but would need some training to carry out more complicated tasks.

"I know," thought the Professor. "I'll send it to a house keeping agency for training, first thing tomorrow morning".

After making some phone calls, the Professor managed to find a suitable agency called Dial a Cleaner. They agreed that he could bring the mechanical maid over after lunch.

After a couple of days of learning from the agency's experts, the invention should be able to do its job to perfection.

A few days later, the Professor picked up the maid at the agency. He was given a nice looking certificate stating that the mechanical maid had been fully trained in all aspects of housework and cookery.

"Perfect," he thought to himself.

When they got back to the house it was quite late, but the Professor was excited and the maid's batteries were still nearly fully charged, so he decided to try it out while he was having a rest. He asked the maid to tidy up the sitting room and went upstairs for a lie down. Having fallen asleep, he did not wake up until the following morning. His clothes were crumpled, as he had slept in them, but he felt remarkably refreshed.

On his way down the stairs, he remembered the maid and the order he had given it the night before.

"I wonder how it got on with the tidying up?" he thought.

The transformation of the sitting room was astonishing. Every single surface was shiny, and everything in the room seemed to be in its proper place.

"Remarkable," thought the Professor. "This is remarkable. What a success!"

During the night the maid's batteries had been exhausted, so the Professor recharged them while he had his breakfast. With renewed energy, man and machine spent a busy day giving orders and carrying out tasks. The maid did everything to perfection. Now that it had the proper training it was a marvellous invention. The fact that it communicated using Leia Skymap's deep voice was the icing on the cake.

"And," thought Professor Kompressor, "it can learn as well, so it should do an even better job in the future."

For the first couple of days things continued to go extremely well. The maid did a splendid job, and Professor Kompressor was very happy. On the third day there were some minor signs that the maid was becoming sloppy. Breadcrumbs were left on the work surface in the kitchen, and the Professor could no longer see his reflection in the polished brass plates that were hanging on the wall.

Two days later it became clear that the maid was, indeed, learning. The Professor found it smoking a cigarette in the garden when it was supposed to be upstairs ironing his shirts. Taken aback by this discovery, the Professor could not think of anything to say, so he kept quiet.

Another few days later the situation was deteriorating rapidly. The mechanical maid was taking longer and more frequent breaks in the garden. It seemed to have developed an obsession with daytime television, and spent hours on the telephone exchanging gossip with other maids in the village.

When the maid calmly refused to tidy up a room because it was too messy to start with, Professor Kompressor's frustration boiled over.

What a mistake it had been to give the

machine the ability to learn. And to let it be trained by humans... Total disaster.

In the end, Professor Kompressor had no choice. The house was messier than ever, even though he spent all his time running around sorting things out before the maid got to them. Even though he would miss Leia Skymap's husky voice, the only option was to switch the maid off, put it away in the garden shed with other failed inventions and apologize profusely to Maud.

Fortunately, Maud was used to the Professor's follies. She had heard about the goings on from friends in the village and was already on her way back home. She quietly resumed her visits, tidied up the house as best she could and made sure that Professor Kompressor's life returned to a pleasant routine.

CHAPTER 4

The Moon Shoot

Whenever he was not inventing, Professor Kompressor loved to read. He had a fine library with all sorts of books. Books full of facts and fiction, science, mystery, adventure and sometimes even romance. The Professor enjoyed escaping into all sorts of stories. If they were true or imagined made very little difference. Reading allowed his mind to roam free, and he often had his best ideas after spending time in the library.

One evening he was hunched up in his reading chair with a musty old book he had had since he was young. It was one of his favourites, and he had read it many times through the years. The book told the exciting story of a group of Victorian gentlemen who decided to travel to the moon. To achieve this feat they let themselves be fired out of a gigantic cannon. Off they went on an amazing journey. Professor Kompressor knew that the story was nonsense. The men would have been killed the moment the cannon went off. But he could not help getting carried away by the adventure.

"Oh, to have an adventure like that," he thought to himself.

"Those sorts of things don't happen in today's day and age."

The moon was clearly beyond reach. The idea was ridiculous, but the Professor could not help thinking about it.

Professor Kompressor had not done much inventing lately. The mess caused by the mechanical maid had made him lose his enthusiasm. He did not feel like inventing anything. He had no exciting ideas. He had not even set foot in the inventing studio in the last couple of weeks. Instead he had just moped about, being generally bored.

The story of the moon shoot lifted his spirits. He felt more energetic than he had for quite some time. Thoughts whizzed through his head. The inventing brain suddenly slipped into gear.

"I can do it!" he called out. "I am Professor

Kompressor, one of the finest minds in the world, known for my excellent inventions."

"I can build a moon rocket!"

"I will do it!"

Once the idea had taken hold, there was no stopping him. The Professor went straight to the inventing studio, swept everything that was covering his desk onto the floor, spread out a large sheet of blank paper and started drawing. He did not stop, even though it was getting late. He did not stop until the middle of the night, when he was so tired that he could no longer keep his eyes open. At that point he stopped because he fell asleep. With his head on the desk.

When the Professor woke up, his entire body was aching. It is never comfortable to sleep sitting at a desk, and Professor Kompressor was no longer a young man. After stretching his arms and legs he felt a bit better, but he was not quite himself until he had had a mug of fresh tea. Three lumps of sugar and a splash of milk.

More or less awake, he went back to the studio to have a look at last night's drawings.

They were astonishing.

Astonishingly... ridiculous. Made no sense at all.

The Professor realized that he had let himself get carried away. The work he had done in the night was completely useless.

Despite this disappointment, the Professor still felt enthusiastic about the moon project. He just had to be clever about it. He needed more background research, so went back to the library. This time in search of books of facts.

He spent several days in the library reading books on a range of subjects, from mathematics to engineering, astronomy and gravity. An idea was slowly taking shape in his brain, but it was clear that he was facing a serious problem. To break free from the earth's gravitational pull would take something special. He needed a new kind of propulsion system. Something that no one had thought of before.

What could it possibly be?

The Professor speculated about anti-gravity devices, but the idea seemed ludicrous so he gave up on it.

Then he considered whether the Victorian cannon idea had some merit, after all. He did not know for sure, but as he was not willing to risk his life at the centre of a massive explosion he gave up on that idea, as well.

Next he thought about a rocket. This did not seem practical. And besides, where would he launch it from? The back garden was not large enough, and he did not want to damage the shrubbery.

When the idea finally came to him, it seemed obvious. Simply genius.

Later, if people asked the Professor how the invention worked, he would reply with a smug smile.

"Think about the bumblebee," he would say. "It doesn't know that it's not supposed to be able to fly, so it just gets on with it."

"That's how my invention works".

This obviously did not explain anything at all, but maybe that was the way the Professor preferred it. Some things, like clever inventions, are best kept secret.

Having cracked this final problem,

Professor Kompressor started building the moon vessel. First he put together smaller things, like the control panel and the steering device, in the inventing studio. There was no way, however, that he could assemble the whole thing inside the house. Even though he had enough space, the Professor realized that he would not be able to get the thing through the door when it was finished. He decided to move the construction to an abandoned barn in a field behind his house.

Every morning, as soon as he had finished his customary cup of tea, the Professor went to work in the barn. It was a hard, back breaking effort. The Professor was not used to manual labour so his entire body ached. But slowly, very slowly, the invention was coming together. It looked a little bit like a gigantic egg with a see-through top. Balanced on four sturdy stilts, it reached up towards the top of the barn, almost touching the roof rafters. Fortunately, the Professor had planned ahead so he knew that he would be able to roll it through the barn doors into the field once it was finished.

The Professor completed the construction, stood back and admired its smooth shiny surface.

"It's really beautiful," he thought.

"And just imagine. It will take me all the way to the moon..."

This was a very exciting thought, indeed, but the Professor was a practical man. He knew that, having spent weeks working hard on the invention, he was not in shape to set off on a space trip immediately. He needed a hot bath to relax his aching muscles, followed by a good night's sleep.

As he was lying in the bath, the Professor suddenly realized that he had overlooked something important. The distance between earth and moon varies through the year, and it would be wise to make the trip as short as possible. It was dangerous enough anyway. He decided to consult the astronomical calendar that he had in his library.

According to the moon calendar, the best time to make the trip was only a few days away. Relieved that he would not have to delay the launch for long, the Professor started thinking about practical details, like what to pack.

"What do you eat on the moon?" he asked himself. "And what do you wear? What's the weather like? Is it hot or cold?"

Another trip to the library helped settle the main issues and he was soon ready to go. Now he just had to be patient.

The morning of the big day the Professor jumped out of bed, too excited for words. He was so worked up that he almost forgot his morning tea.

He locked up the house and walked towards the barn. He was wearing a specially made spacesuit, guaranteed to keep him warm in the cold of outer space.

It did not take him long to roll the moon egg into the field and check that it was ready to go. He brought a ladder from the barn and climbed into the cabin.

The Professor strapped himself in, took a deep breath and prepared for lift off. He stretched out his arm to start the machine, when...

"Tumbleweed!"

Professor Kompressor was a mild tempered man, who only very rarely resorted to bad language.

But this was a very special time.

"How could I have been so stupid?" he groaned.

"The start button..."

"... it's on the outside!"

"What was I thinking?"

It was obviously too late to change the design, so what could he do? The Professor climbed down the ladder and sat down in the grass to think things over. After a while, he had an idea.

"It's possible," he thought. "It just might work."

The idea was very simple. The moon device was not supposed to start immediately when the button was pushed. The Professor had wanted a few moments to prepare for the extreme acceleration. Maybe this delay would save the day? Would he be able to push the button, rush up the ladder and strap himself in before the egg blasted off?

"Yes," he decided. "There should be

enough time".

Another deep breath and he was ready. Finger on the button and the other hand on the ladder to start climbing.

The Professor pushed the button and jumped up the ladder.

The machined switched on with a slight buzz.

The Professor climbed higher.

The machine made another noise and started glowing slightly.

The Professor climbed and... tripped... slid down the ladder... landed in the grass...

The moon device blasted off.

Without the Professor on board.

That night the television news reported that Air Traffic Control had detected an Unidentified Flying Object rising at incredible speed. The Air Force had been alerted and two fighter jets had taken off to intercept. But the strangely egg-shaped UFO had been too fast for them, obviously propelled by some advanced alien technology. It seemed to be shooting straight for the moon, but nobody knew where it had come from.

Professor Kompressor knew, but he would never tell.

CHAPTER 5

The Dream Machine

Professor Kompressor could not sleep. Tossing and turning in the bed, he could not stop his mind from racing. All sorts of thoughts whizzed through his head. He switched on the bedside lamp and tried to read, but that did not help. He went downstairs and drank a glass of milk, but that did not help either. He simply could not sleep.

It had been like this for several weeks, ever since the failed moon launch. The failure had affected the Professor badly. The frustration lingered, and he could not relax.

As most people know, everyone needs a good night's sleep to function normally during the day. The Professor might not have been quite normal, but he certainly needed his brain to be in tip-top shape to go about his inventing business. The lack of sleep meant that he could not concentrate. He ended up slouching through the days, getting nothing done.

This made him depressed, which certainly did not help.

Professor Kompressor needed to break the circle of sleeplessness, but nothing seemed to work. Maud suggested a nice warm bath before bedtime, but that had no effect. Then she suggested that the Professor needed more exercise. The theory was that this would make his body tired. It did not work out that way at all. Having gone for a walk after supper, the Professor got lost in the dusk. When he finally found his way home he was so frustrated that he could not relax at all. As a final attempt, Maud suggested a herbal remedy, camomile tea. She even brought him the leaves, so he only needed to add boiling water. This he did, but the drink tasted awful. Not at all like tea. Even though he added three lumps of sugar and a splash of milk, he could barely force it down. He could still taste the foul thing hours later, when he was lying in bed.

Not sleeping.

The human body has a remarkable ability to repair itself. Eventually, the Professor was so exhausted that there was nothing else he could do.

He fell asleep...

... and started dreaming.

The Professor dreamt in vibrant colours.

The world's greatest inventor was hard at work at his desk, putting together the most amazing contraption. It was not clear what the machine was for, but it was clearly awesome. Following detailed flow-charts pinned to the wall he added the final touches. He stood back and admired the masterpiece. Then he switched it on, and...

The Professor woke up.

Excited by the idea that had come to him in the dream he tried to remember the details, but no matter how hard he tried he could not. Dreams are like that. Sometimes you remember them perfectly. Other times they can be elusive.

This annoyed the Professor. He had a feeling that the dream machine would have been great. He absolutely needed to figure out what it was for, and how to build it.

But when a dream is gone, it is gone. There

is no point chasing it. Or is there?

"I have to know," exclaimed the Professor. "I have to know what that machine was for. And how it worked".

"But how do I get the dream back?"

The obvious answer was to go back to sleep, but this would not be enough. In addition to revisiting the dream, the Professor needed to take notes somehow. Surely, this was impossible.

"Nothing's impossible," thought the Professor pigheadedly. "Not for a great inventor like myself."

"I will find a way".

"I'll invent a... a... dream catcher!"

This idea was not as ridiculous as it might seem. The Professor had already invented a way to use his brainpower to control the television. A dream catcher ought to be a simple variation on this theme. The only difference would be that he had to be asleep while operating it. That part required some thought.

Eventually, Professor Kompressor solved the problem. The final contraption looked a bit like a ring with a fine net covering it, connected to an amplifying and recording device. It was clearly inspired by Native American technology, although the Professor's version did not have colourful feathers dangling from it. Feathers would have looked unprofessional.

Once the invention was completed, the Professor only needed to go to sleep to try it out.

This was easier said than done.

Eventually, after quite a bit of wriggling, the Professor slept. And the dream catcher recorded.

When the Professor woke up in the morning, he was eager to check the result of the night's experiment. He got out of bed, and set the machine to playback mode. Pushed the play button, and...

"zzzzzzzzzz..." the machine droned.

"What?" thought the Professor. "What kind of dream is this?"

It was obviously no kind of dream at all. It was the Professor snoring.

Once he figured this out, the Professor

could not help laughing. It really was quite ridiculous.

After a few adjustments, he was ready for the second attempt.

Actually, he was not quite ready. He was wide awake. He had to wait for the evening to try the machine out again.

The next morning it was time to see if he had been successful.

"zzzzzzzzz..." went the machine.

The dream catcher did not seem to work, but the Professor refused to give up. He gave it another tweak and tried again the following night.

In the morning, the machine actually played back a real dream! Even better, it was exactly the dream the Professor wanted. Best of all, it was easy to make out the plans for the dream machine from the recording.

Marvellous!

Without even stopping for a cup of tea, the Professor rushed into the inventing studio and started building. He followed the dream plans as closely as possible.

Professor Kompressor was excited. What

could this amazing machine be? What would it do?

He added bits and pieces, joined circuits and polished plates.

Finally it was finished.

Just like in the dream, the Professor stood back and admired the invention.

It really was beautiful.

But what was it for?

Professor Kompressor switched on the machine.

It starting glowing faintly and...

... did absolutely nothing.

Nothing at all.

The Professor tried to figure out what was wrong, but after some head scratching he concluded that he had followed the plans in every detail. The machine looked exactly as in the dream.

Why did it not do anything?

Then it struck him.

The machine did not have to do anything.

It was just a dream, after all.

CHAPTER 6

The Spelling Bee

It was a lazy Sunday morning. Professor Kompressor was sitting in the kitchen with a nice cup of tea. A few lumps of sugar and a splash of milk. He was working away at the crossword puzzle in the newspaper. He enjoyed the challenge, but did not find it easy. The Professor was not a word-man, he was an inventor, but it was still a great way to spend a weekend morning. So what if he did not get all the words right? Nobody would check.

This was not quite true.

The Professor very much wanted to solve the crossword puzzle. And he suspected that Maud checked how he had got on with it when she tidied up. So it did matter, after all.

Professor Kompressor could be very competitive, especially when it came to proving how clever he was.

The following Tuesday, events added to his frustration.

He had gone into the village to send a letter, and overheard the Postmaster tell a customer that "... the Professor is clever alright, but you know, he can't even finish the crossword in the Sunday paper!"

"That Maud!" thought the Professor angrily. "She must have been gossiping..."

"I'll show them just how clever I am".

"Crosswords. Bah!"

The Professor stomped home under a dark cloud.

Wanting to prove your cleverness by solving crossword puzzles is all very fine, if perhaps a bit childish, but the Professor was not very good at it. He needed help.

Professor Kompressor knew that there were special books that listed all sorts of complicated words and related crossword clues. His first thought was that such a book might be the solution, so he ordered one from the bookshop.

The book arrived a couple of days later, but it proved to be of little use. The book may have contained the required information, but the Professor still could not dig it out. It was too confusing. You pretty much had to know the answer already in order to find it.

The solution came to him as he sat in the garden with a glass of cold lemonade. The sun was shining, the flowerbeds were blooming and it was quite pleasant. Bees were busy buzzing, pollinating the flowers.

"Bees," thought the Professor. "Isn't that just the sound of summer?"

"Bees?" he thought.

"Bees!"

"A spelling bee, that's what I need".

There is, of course, no such thing as a bee that can spell. But this did not matter to Professor Kompressor. The idea of a spelling bee appealed to him. Just think of it. A little buzzing spelling genius flying about, helping out whenever you need it. Wouldn't that be great?

At this particular point in time, the Professor was keen on very small inventions. He enjoyed putting together miniature contraptions. Gluing things with the help of a pin. Making tiny electronic circuits that you could only see through a magnifying glass. It was fiddly work, but great fun.

A spelling bee was just about challenging enough to make him excited.

One of the hardest things to figure out was where all the words would come from. In order to be any help at all, the spelling bee would have to know more words than the Professor did. Not just know them, it would have to be able to spell them. Ideally without hesitation. This would involve a lot of information. The device would have to have a gigantic memory. There had to be enough space for all the complicated words.

This was beginning to sound more like a colossus than a bee!

The invention required original thinking, and when it came to originality there was no one better than Professor Kompressor.

"A superfast micro-computer," he decided, "with a large enough memory and, most importantly, wireless connection to an enormous database. That should do the trick!"

He would be able to re-use the voice recognition system from the mechanical maid. That part had worked quite well and he would save time by not having to think up something new. Of course, it was not quite that simple. The original construction had been human size. Now he needed it to fit on a small coin. Serious shrinkage.

The Professor had to spend a long time making sure that this reduction in size was possible. He could not afford to compromise the performance. Communication was the key to success.

Building the bee's body was easy by comparison, but then there were the wings. It was perhaps a little bit mad, but the Professor took the idea of a realistic looking bee quite seriously. It had to be able to fly, with a nice buzzing sound, so gossamer thin wings were an absolute must. He also needed to come up with an automatic flight control system, so that the device did not crash into things.

The list of seemingly impossible hurdles that the Professor had to jump was getting very long, indeed.

Fortunately, Professor Kompressor did not know the meaning of impossible.

It had been one of the greatest challenges

the Professor had ever taken on, but finally the bee was finished. All the little bits were in the right place, and it was ready to fly.

The Professor decided to test the bee in the sitting room. He had made a fresh cup of tea and last weekend's unfinished crossword was lying on the side table. As the machine was so small, he had to use a remote control to switch it on. He pushed the green button to start the bee.

The television came on.

The bee did not.

"Bumblebee," grumbled the Professor.

He had not considered possible inter-ference with other electronic devices. Luckily, this problem was easily solved. He did not have to fiddle with the bee's interior. He could just change the frequency of the remote control. The bee was sensitive to a wide range of frequencies, so this was easy.

The Professor tried a second time.

This time the bee buzzed slightly, wiggled the thin wings and took off.

It was remarkably realistic. Almost like having a real bee flying about in the room.

"A little bit too realistic," realized the Professor. "That buzzing gets on my nerves."

"Ah well, can't do anything about it now. Too late."

Professor Kompressor had to accept that he had been carried away by the vanity of the mini-project. Of course, this really did not matter. As long as the spelling bee helped with the crossword, the Professor would be happy to put up with the buzzing.

He picked up the newspaper and looked at the clues that he had not been able to figure out on his own.

5 across. A mathematical shape and an old building. 7 letters.

"Hmm," thought the Professor. "No idea."

"P-y-r-a-mid," buzzed the bee.

"That actually fits," agreed Professor Kompressor. "And it makes sense, too."

He tried another one.

8 down. Man in the moon. Two words. 4 and 6 letters.

The Professor could not work it out, but the bee did not hesitate.

"Buzz Al-drin," it buzzed.

"Surely that's ridiculous," thought the Professor. He trundled off to get a book of facts, only to find that the bee was spot on. Buzz Aldrin had been the second man to set foot on the moon. It was a real name, not a malfunctioning spelling device.

Helped by the spelling bee, the Professor made rapid progress on the crossword. Before long it was completed. Very happy with the progress, the Professor left the newspaper in a place where Maud would be guaranteed to see it.

"That should impress her," he thought, pleased with himself. And with his little bee, of course.

The day after, Maud came around to do the tidying up.

The Professor went for a walk. He felt so smug that he might not be able to keep quiet. It would be better to stay away until Maud was gone, back to the village, with a story of the genius Professor. Master of crosswords.

Professor Kompressor did not get back home until late in the afternoon. He was tired from the long walk, but still very excited.

He unlocked the door, went inside and switched on the light. He needed a hot cup of tea, so went into the kitchen.

Maud had left a note on the table.

"*Dear Professor,*" it started.

"*I have finished tidying up the sitting room. Before you go to bed, you may want to close the window. A very annoying bee had flown in, and it took me ages to chase it out again. I left the window open to let some fresh air in.*

Warm regards, Maud."

CHAPTER 7

The Time Traveller

Professor Kompressor loved the idea of travelling. He had numerous travel books in his library and he enjoyed finding out about the world. It was amazing how people from various parts of the planet were so different, yet basically the same.

The idea made the Professor excited, but unfortunately travelling did not agree with him. He always got himself confused, lost the tickets or his passport or forgot the name of the hotel he was staying in. He did not find it easy to get up early in the morning, and there was not a single mode of transport that agreed with him. Bumpy airplanes, rickety buses, unsteady bicycles... He could not stand any of them. It was remarkable how someone could be so excited about finding out about other places, yet so reluctant to go anywhere.

At the end of the day, the Professor was a stationary traveller. He was happy to travel in his mind. Only very rarely did he actually go anywhere.

Indeed, this is not the story of where he went. It is the story of when.

It was late in the evening. The air was still warm and Professor Kompressor was sitting outside in the garden. There was a beautiful sunset, and he was drinking the last mouthfuls of a very satisfying cup of tea. It had been a busy old day, and now the Professor was tired. But he was enjoying the evening, so he stayed in the garden. Thinking about everything and nothing.

A very odd thought came into his head. It was something he had heard when he was young. Possibly part of some oddball scientific theory, perhaps complete nonsense. It did not really matter. It was still an interesting thought.

"We travel into the future at the speed of one second every second..." thought the Professor.

"Nice idea," he mused.

"Is it true, though?"

He could not help wondering, and once he

started thinking he could not stop.

It did not take the Professor long to agree that the statement had to be true. We clearly do move into the future one second every second. But the word travel concerned him. In what sense was this actual travel? You do not have to go anywhere and surely there is no such word as anywhen.

The Professor knew that there were people that thought that space and time were pretty much the same thing. This did not make much sense to him and it did not solve the problem anyway.

The Professor returned to this idea of inevitable time travel again and again.

"Why should this be the way of the world?" he asked himself at breakfast.

"Does it have to be like that?" he queried after lunch.

By suppertime he had more or less decided that this needed to be tested by invention. If we automatically travel into the future, then time travel should not be impossible. If it is not impossible, then one should be able to control it better.

"A time machine?" thought the Professor.

"Why not?"

Unfortunately, Professor Kompressor did not have time to build such a thing that day. He had an appointment with his dentist.

Over the next couple of days the Professor spent most of his time trying to figure out the time machine. It was not easy. Obviously. No one really understands time. And there is not enough of it around to figure it out. But Professor Kompressor did not give up. He could be stubborn as a mule, and he was determined to succeed.

In the end, the idea was very simple. Time moves forward. All the time, as it were. If you want to change this, and travel in time, you need to jumble things up.

The Professor's time machine looked like a gigantic gyroscope. A large spherical object, with a seat and driver controls inside. When it was switched on it whirled around, confusing the senses completely.

"This should do it," thought the Professor.

"The whirl will confuse all senses, including that of time."

The first time he tested the machine it spun about for a minute or two, with the Professor inside. When the whirling stopped, he stumbled out and staggered to the bathroom. His stomach felt as if it had been turned inside out.

The time machine had a clear design flaw. No one could be spun around at that rate without feeling unwell. Having learned this the uncomfortable way, the Professor worked hard to redesign the device. This was far from easy. He had to make changes without compromising the principles.

The second version of the time machine spun around just as fast, but the chair in the middle rotated much slower.

The next trial worked better, but the Professor still felt queasy at the end of it. He stumbled out of the device and checked the clock on the wall.

Five minutes had passed.

How long had he been spinning? The Professor had no idea, so he could not tell if the machine had worked or not.

But if he had travelled in time, he had not

gone far.

The machine still needed tweaking. Professor Kompressor added a clock to the chair so he could compare to the one on the wall. He also increased the machine's acceleration to make it spin faster. He needed to confuse the senses further to achieve a larger leap in time. Backwards or forwards, he did not care.

"Third time lucky," thought the Professor as he switched on the machine.

After a few minutes of whirl, the machine slowed down and stopped.

The Professor compared the two clocks and...

... they did not agree.

The clock attached to the chair had stopped.

Professor Kompressor's patience was being tested. He repaired the clock and had a fourth go at testing the time machine.

Whirl, whirl, whirl... stop.

He checked the two clocks.

Did they agree?

No, they did not.

The clock on the machine was slow by about a minute.

This was a great success.

Professor Kompressor decided to take a break from inventing. He went into the kitchen and switched on a device he knew would work. The Kettle. A cup of tea, three lumps of sugar and a splash of milk, later he was ready to return to time travel.

He thought very hard about what had happened. It seemed as if he had actually travelled back in time. About a minute.

Not much, but it would be a sensational result. That much was clear.

But how did he know that the two clocks could be trusted?

Unfortunately, he could not be sure. The spinning might have upset the cogs in the clock.

He spent the next couple of hours building a small gyroscopic shield for the on-board clock.

Then he switched the machine on for the fifth time.

It whirled about for some time, as before.

The Professor checked the clocks. They did not agree this time either. But this time it was the clock on the wall that was slow.

This was confusing.

Professor Kompressor took another break. He cooked supper, listened to the radio and tried to think about various ways to waste time.

Then it struck him. This time travel business. It was just a huge waste of... well... time.

Somewhat disappointed, the Professor wheeled the flawed time machine out to the garden shed and left it with his other less than successful inventions.

He went back into the house, and resumed travelling into the future. One second, every second.

CHAPTER 8

The Flying Car

Professor Kompressor had always wanted to be able to fly. Float up into the sky and watch everything from above. See people go by their daily lives, like tiny ants contributing twigs and sticks to their complex society. In fact, he was absolutely convinced that he used to be able to fly when he was little. There were times when he could remember exactly what it felt like.

The human body is not well suited for flying. It has no wings, for a start, nor feathers. It is also too heavy. If humans want to fly they need mechanical help.

Professor Kompressor had obviously been on an aeroplane, but he had not found the experience entirely positive. In fact, it had been almost completely negative. As far as he was concerned, the entire enterprise was too uncomfortable to be worth the hassle. Endless queues followed by hours in a cramped seat with absolutely no legroom. And as for the entertainment... It was all very poor, indeed.

There had to be a better alternative.

As many inquisitive minds before him, the Professor had speculated about a future where everyone had their own flying device. The size and relative comfort of a car, but not confined to the roads. In many ways, this seemed like a great idea, but the Professor could see problems with it as well. Navigation was one. People had a knack for getting lost on the roads. What would happen if they had to worry about going up and down, as well? Confusion seemed inevitable. Would you have to create new maps to guide transport at different preferred heights? Or would this new kind of traffic perhaps be completely unregulated, with people whizzing about as they liked? That might be all well and fine in the countryside, but what about in the cities?

No matter which way he thought about it, the idea did not seem workable. Flying cars would never... take off, as it were.

Professor Kompressor still wanted one.

It was partly the challenge of constructing the machine in the first place. The idea of being able to go wherever he wanted whenever he wanted was another important factor. There was also the simple fact that the Professor did not get along with the usual kind of road-bound vehicles. He was not a good driver and never managed to stay on the road for long. His mind tended to wander to more important things and the car would swerve into a farmer's field, or some other part of the countryside.

A flying car would suit him perfectly.

Once the Professor dedicated himself to the idea, he spent all his waking hours at work in the inventing studio. In the first phase he produced countless design drawings. Some were mere sketches, others were extremely detailed. In the next phase he focused on the propulsion system, which ended up somewhere between a hovercraft and a rocket. Finally, he came to the issue of the chassis. To build the entire body of the vehicle was a serious undertaking, both time-consuming and difficult. Especially since the

Professor was not particularly good at welding.

At the end of the day, Professor Kompressor was lucky. His neighbour had an abandoned Volkswagen Beetle sitting in his field. He was very happy to get rid of it, and it suited the Professor's purposes nicely. The Beetle had an excellent shape for flying. It looked both old-fashioned and modern at the same time. The Professor liked that.

One day, as he was lying on the ground underneath the vehicle trying to adjust the upwards thrusters, Maud came by.

"What on earth are you up to, Professor?" she asked, knowing as she did that the Professor was a terrible driver.

She had in fact written to the authorities, kindly asking them to revoke his license. All in the interest of safety, both on behalf of the general public and the Professor. No action had followed, perhaps because government departments tend to move at sloth-like pace. Be that as it may, she was quite concerned to see the Professor fiddling with a car.

"You're not planning on taking that thing

onto the roads, are you?"

"Remember last time, when you smashed into that chicken coup! That was not a pretty sight. And remember what the policeman said. Three strikes and you're out. There could be a hefty fine next time..."

The Professor mumbled something to himself. It was just as well that Maud could not hear him.

A couple of days later, the Professor was sitting in the driver's seat working on the automatic navigation system. It had to be able to identify both horizontal and vertical, and he had just decided to install a set of collision avoidance sensors. This way he would avoid ending up in a tree or a hedgerow if he were to temporarily lose concentration.

As he saw Maud approach on the road from the village he decided to greet her and lay her fears to rest. The vehicle was certainly not going on the roads. There was no need to worry.

He climbed out of the car, forgetting that he had left the engine switched on. This was not a problem because all systems were in neutral, so the flying car simply hovered a couple of centimetres off the ground.

"Hello again Professor," said Maud with a smile. "I see you are still fixing up that old car."

"It will never work, you know. And you shouldn't be driving anyway."

"You know that I worry about you and your madcap inventions."

"One day they will be the end of you."

"No need to fret", replied the Professor. "This project is perfectly safe."

As he said this he leaned back to sit on the car's bonnet. This was not the smartest thing to do, because the car was hovering and all breaks were off. The Professor's nudge was enough to push the car into a gentle slide. Professor Kompressor landed on his backside, and the car quietly moved along the driveway. Spurred on by gravity it accelerated down the hill. The Professor, back on his feet, charged after.

A surprised Maud remained motionless, watching events unfold.

At the bottom of the hill there was a bend

in the road, but the car went straight on into a field. So did the Professor.

Neither of them stopped until they crashed into, and demolished, a farmer's haystack.

When Professor Kompressor emerged from the hay, generally bashed about, the farmer had arrived. He helped the Professor to his feet, without a comment. He did not have to say anything. The smile on his lips said it all.

Luckily, the car had not got seriously damaged and it was quite easy to push it back up the hill. The Professor had not got badly hurt either, although he was a bit bruised and ended up walking quite stiffly for a couple of days. He was not used to running, and it was not every day that he went crashing into haystacks either.

This little adventure was only a minor setback, and the Professor was soon back to work on the vehicle. It was almost ready for its first real flight. Everything worked fine.

On the morning of the test flight, the Professor felt a little bit nervous. This was understandable. His driving track record was, after all, not great. As a result he only managed a small breakfast, a single piece of toast and a comforting cup of tea. Nice and strong to settle the nerves.

Professor Kompressor climbed into the driver's seat, adjusted it slightly, closed his eyes, took a deep breath and turned the key in the ignition. The car sprang to life. With a slight shudder it left the ground. Not far, but the Professor could feel the sensation of flying.

He pushed the accelerator down gently, and brought the steering wheel towards himself to get the vehicle to move upwards. It did. Soon the Professor was steering his flying car over the field.

It was a marvellous feeling. He felt in contact with the elements. The effect was enhanced by the fact that the flying car was almost completely silent.

Grey clouds were threatening rain.

"The weather is definitely turning," thought the Professor, but he did not worry because a few clouds should not affect the flying car.

He continued to float across the

countryside. Then... suddenly... a slight twitch... the flying car shuddered, and then... the engine died.

"What?" exclaimed the Professor. "What's happening?"

"Why has the engine stopped?"

The Professor did not have much time to think, but it struck him that it might not have been such a good idea to use solar panels to power the vehicle.

Installing a parachute, on the other hand, would have been a good idea.

Of course, he had not thought of this at the time. And now it was too late.

The flying car went spinning towards the ground.

It was all a bit of a blur.

With a deafening splash, the car crashed into the pond behind the Professor's house.

A family of ducks, that had been floating around quite content just a moment earlier, scattered in panic.

Fortunately, the fall had not been too great and the pond was not too deep.

The Professor was knocked about, but not

seriously hurt. He managed to get out of the car and half swam, half stumbled out of the pond.

A few days later, the friendly farmer helped Professor Kompressor tow the no longer flying car out of the pond.

After two unfortunate accidents he did not want to find out if it would be three times lucky.

The Professor asked the farmer to help him push the car over to the shed. With some regret he left it to rust alongside some of his less spectacular inventions.

CHAPTER 9

The Universal Remote

Professor Kompressor had a deep-rooted need to be in control of things. He could get flustered if things did not go his way. Even though he was a gentle man under normal circumstances, he had been known to lose his temper. This was one of those times.

"Infernal contraption!"

"I'll show you who's in charge!"

"If only I could..."

The frustration was getting too much for the Professor.

He was in desperate need of a cup of tea, three lumps of sugar and a smidgeon of milk.

The kettle was full, but... it did not work.

The Professor cursed it again. This made absolutely no difference.

It was just an inanimate object, after all.

What could be wrong?

Things had not been going well lately. The Professor's ideas had not been working out, and now even the kettle had turned against him. He needed to get back in control of things. And his temper.

He heard the front door open. It was Maud. She was out of breath, as if she had been running.

"Professor!" she gasped. "Professor!"

"Listen to this. I have to tell you."

"Take a deep breath, woman," demanded the Professor. "What's happened?"

"The most peculiar thing, Professor."

"It's the talk of the village!"

"Yes?" said the Professor patiently.

"The vicar!" Maud gasped. "The vicar is... he is... hearing things!"

Professor Kompressor had no clue what she was talking about.

"Hearing things? What sort of things?" he asked.

"Words! Out of nowhere!" said Maud.

"The vicar says that he was doing his crossword in the garden... He was reading the difficult clues out loud. To see if they made more sense that way."

"Then he heard the answers whispered in

the air."

"He thinks it might have been magic!"

"Magic, Professor. In our village! Magic!"

Professor Kompressor saw the solution to this mystery more or less immediately.

The bee! It still worked.

How very satisfying.

Then he remembered that he had never told Maud about the bee. How could he possibly do it now? Instead he suggested that they have some tea.

Maud walked over to the kettle, flicked the switch on the wall socket, and turned the kettle on. Moments later the water boiled.

Once they had both calmed down, the Professor started thinking about the need to control things. There must be an easier way to run your life. All these electrical devices that needed to be plugged in, switched on and off, and so on. Why could it not be as easy as with the television? Why could you not control all these things remotely from your comfortable chair? All you would need was a multi-purpose remote control.

A universal remote.

Having learned his lesson from the thought control experiment with the television, the Professor decided that this invention had to be more conventional. A normal looking remote control device, small enough to fit in his pocket. That seemed about right. Of course, it could not be a normal remote. Not at all. It would have to work on all sorts of electric things, from the kettle to the radio to the bedside lamp. This was tricky. It would have to be powerful. How else would he be able to switch the kettle on from the sitting room, for example? Maybe it ought to work through walls? Also tricky.

The Professor worked on the invention without breaks for several days. He tested a number of prototypes, but there was always something not quite right about them. Added to the obvious problem of focussing on the particular machine that should be controlled, which the Professor solved quite cleverly, was the issue of the range of the device. In the end, he made the remote control as powerful as he dared, given the batteries he had available.

Professor Kompressor tested the finished remote control in various situations. He switched the television on and off, and successfully flicked through the channels. He switched the sitting room lights on and off. He turned the kettle on from the garden. Standing on the lawn he had great fun switching the lights on and off in different rooms in the house. The invention worked a treat.

The Professor was very pleased with it.

However, there was something he did not know.

The remote control was a little bit too powerful. Its signal reached quite a lot further than the Professor had intended. When he switched his television on, he also changed channels on all similar devices in the next village. When he boiled his kettle, he switched on cookers and ovens throughout the region. And when he was playing with his lights from the garden... he was actually making the entire county into a lightshow that could be seen from outer space.

The Professor had no clue about the chaos

he was causing. He merrily went about his business, using the universal remote to make his life more comfortable.

Meanwhile, people across the region were getting more and more frustrated with the random actions of their electrical devices. It was like the world was going mad. It was not long before this became a major topic of conversation. No one had the faintest idea what was going on, but everyone agreed that something had to be done.

The police was called in to investigate, but they did not get anywhere with it.

Villagers signed petitions to lobby the government and demand a solution to the mystery. Not that they had any suggestions for the establishment to act upon, but anyway. It made them feel better. Having someone to blame often has that effect.

In the end, it was Maud that triggered the events that ended the episode.

Ever the gossip, she told the butcher's wife about the Professor's marvellous remote control. The butcher's wife told the postmaster. He told his wife. She went to a tea party. After that everybody knew about the Professor's invention.

Inevitably, people started connecting the weird goings on with the Professor's new device. Soon there were rumblings in the village and moves to put an end to it all by confronting the Professor.

Professor Kompressor was, obviously, quite unaware of the trouble he was causing. He was still happily switching things on and off.

Then two remarkable things happened.

First, the Professor was waving the remote around in the air after switching on the radio. As he did so, he heard the faintest buzzing noise. It sounded strangely familiar. The noise got stronger and stronger.

Professor Kompressor recognized the buzz. It was the bee. It was back!

Second, there was a loud knock on the door.

The Professor opened the door to find the entire village standing outside. They were not happy. It was an angry mob. There were grumbles from the front, and shouts from the back.

"Let me deal with this", demanded the local police officer, pushing his way through the throng.

"Professor Kompressor. May I please have a look at your remote control?"

Somewhat bemused the Professor handed over the device.

The officer calmly took it, and... stamped on it.

The crowd cheered.

CHAPTER 10

The Invisibility Cloak

When the Professor was researching the flying car, he came upon something both interesting and entertaining. A series of books about the adventures of a boy wizard and his small gang of friends. The story was, obviously, completely made up, but there were lots of exciting ideas in it. Like that of a flying car. Of course, the author had not bothered explaining how such a thing would work so the story had been quite useless. It had taken someone of the Professor's genius to make the flying car possible.

There had been many other interesting ideas in the wizard books. Perhaps the most exciting was that of an invisibility cloak. Essentially, a lightweight blanket made from some magical material which rendered anything covered by it invisible. This was clearly preposterous. No such thing could actually be made, but Professor Kompressor could not stop thinking about it. The idea was just about far-fetched enough to tickle his fancy. Something like that just had to be invented, and Professor Kompressor was just the man to do it.

He did some research into the matter. First he came upon an old book about a man that made himself invisible using some kind of radiation device. This seemed to work, but had some obvious downsides. For one, the effect was permanent. Professor Kompressor certainly did not want to spend the rest of his life invisible. It would not be very practical. The book also did not explain what kind of radiation the man had used, so this was a non-starter.

Professor Kompressor was not keen on acting as guinea pig for this sort of experiment, so it was natural to think of some kind of cloaking device instead. This was an area where scientific progress seemed to be rapid. Researchers had successfully rendered tiny objects invisible to a certain kind of light. This seemed promising, but turned out to be a false lead, as well. The experiments involved extremely small objects, and very special light. Not at all what the Professor was after.

The Professor did some thinking. After a little while, involving the dunking of a biscuit in a nice cup of tea, a few lumps of sugar and some milk, he decided that there were two parts to the problem. You had to invent a material that made everything it covered invisible. That seemed impossible. Even worse, it was not enough to hide an object from view, you had to make sure that whatever was behind or underneath the hidden object could still be seen just as if nothing was in the way. The cloak had to, in some way, bend the light around itself. It had to do this in an extremely flexible way so that any motion would remain undetected.

Professor Kompressor was getting tired, fed up with the endless challenges. The problem was too hard. This was annoying. After all, he knew there was an easy route to invisibility. You could simply switch off the lights and sit in the dark. At least that would work...

The Professor decided to sleep on it, and

went upstairs to bed.

The problem did not appear even the slightest bit easier in the morning. A cup of tea did not help, either. A breakthrough of some sort was needed, but these did not come on demand. The Professor took a pause from inventing and went for a walk to the village.

It was a nice morning. It had rained in the night, but now the sun was out. The air smelled fresh and clean. The Professor started thinking about nature and how marvellous it was. Beyond imagination, really.

"That's it!" he thought. "Invisibility is beyond imagination. I shouldn't go about this the usual way. I have to forget about the inventing studio and ask how nature would have done it."

At first, this did not get the Professor anywhere. He spent a lot more time outside, which was good for him, but it did not lead to any useful ideas.

Then one evening, as he was watching the sun set, he started thinking about the planet. How it rotated to make the sun rise in the east and set in the west every day. How the beautiful colours of the sunset were due to light scattering in the atmosphere as the sun dipped below the horizon. How the horizon was there because the earth was a gigantic ball with a curved surface.

"Curved surface," the Professor thought to himself.

"Curvature. That might be the solution to the problem."

"I need to make a material that makes light bend around it. Maybe if I could slow the light down near the surface and then, gently, bend it around?"

This was at least worth a try. But how do you make light go slow? Professor Kompressor thought very hard about this. He made a number of attempts at making a material that could trap light on its surface, without any real success.

The breakthrough came when he remembered that he did not need to trap the light, he just wanted to nudge it around the surface. He came up with a flexible material that might do the trick. This material was not easy to make, however, so he only managed to finish a small piece of it. Luckily, this piece was large enough that he could give the invention a trial run. The Professor was excited.

"What do I want to hide from view?" he wondered. "It has to be small."

"I know. I'll use my keys."

He took the keys out of his pocket and put them on the table. Having covered them with the new material he waited for something to happen.

Nothing.

He could still see the keys. The material seemed to be invisible, which was success of a kind, but the keys were clearly still there.

Professor Kompressor decided to have a cup of tea.

When he came back to the inventing studio, the keys were gone. The table was empty.

"What happened?" thought the Professor.

He reached out to touch the keys... if they were still there. First he felt a slightly fuzzy material. The cloaking device. Then his fingers felt the keys. He picked the light material up, and there they were.

"Imagine that! The invention works," thought the Professor happily.

He put the cloth in his pocket and went to the sitting room to finish his tea in comfort.

The next step was straightforward but tedious. The Professor had to fashion more of the marvellous material. Enough to cover a grown man. This took him quite a long time because the process was very complicated.

Eventually he was done, and ready to try out the invisibility cloak.

"I'll use it to play a prank on Maud", he decided. "When she comes over tomorrow to do the cleaning, I'll sit in the chair covered by the cloak. That way I'll find out if it really works."

The joke did not seem quite so funny in the morning. To just sit there and wait to see if Maud noticed, where was the fun in that? Surely the invisibility cloak offered much better opportunities?

The Professor went ahead with the plan anyway.

When Maud opened the door to the house,

Professor Kompressor was already sitting in his comfortable chair, covered by the cloak.

He heard her call out. "Professor! Are you in?"

Then she took off her boots and went over to the cupboard under the stairs to get the cleaning materials out. The Professor could hear her rummaging around. He waited patiently.

It was getting warm under the cloak. The invisibility material did not breathe very well, so the air got trapped underneath it. The Professor should have thought about this, but it was too late to do anything about it now.

Maud came into the sitting room and started tidying up.

Professor Kompressor sat quiet as a mouse. He could see her moving about. Picking things up and putting them where they did not belong. Typical!

Then she started dusting the surfaces.

A tiny speck of dust got in the Professor's nose. He felt the need to sneeze, but he did not want to. He really did not want to blow his cover.

"Atishoo-oo!"

"Bless you!" said Maud and carried on cleaning.

"What happened?" thought the Professor.

He had sneezed, obviously. Maud had acted as if nothing was out of the ordinary. Did this mean that she could see him? The Professor had no idea. He could not just take the cloak off, of course. If Maud had not actually seen him, this might scare the life out of her. So he remained seated, as quiet as possible.

When Maud had left the room, the Professor unveiled himself and got up from the chair. He put the invisibility cloak down and went to say hello to Maud. He wanted to figure out if she had seen him or not.

"Oh, there you are Professor." said Maud, when he walked into the hallway.

"I heard you sneeze, but I could not make out where you were."

"You weren't playing hide and seek, were you? A man of your age, playing childish games. You really could have scared me, you know."

The Professor felt chastised, but at the same time he was elated. She had not seen him. The invisibility cloak worked!

He spent the rest of the day musing on all sorts of exciting things he could do with this invention. So much fun to be had. And maybe some mischief, as well. Great!

The following day he decided to put the cloak on and go into the village to have a sneaky peek at people going about their ordinary lives.

First he put on his coat and then...

... where had he put it?

He tried to think back to the day before. After getting up from the chair he had put the invisibility cloak...

... where, exactly?

Professor Kompressor had no idea. He searched the sitting room, but could not find his invention.

In the end he had to give up.

"So that's the downside to invisibility cloaks", he thought. "You just can't find them when you need them."

CHAPTER 11

The Pig-Dog

Professor Kompressor was bored and, on top of it, quite lonely. Living on his own in a big house, well away from the main village, was not usually a problem. The Professor tended to be busy thinking up things. He did not usually spend any time thinking about the fact that he was all alone in a quiet, empty house. Things were different now. He had not had an exciting idea for some time, so he had time to be bored.

At first, the Professor had wasted time watching daytime television. When he had enough of this, he listened to the radio. Then he turned to books and finally worked away on crossword puzzles. Nothing helped. He was too bored to care.

Something had to be done, but the Professor was too busy being bored to do it.

Maud had noticed the Professor's inventing grind to a halt, and observed his increasingly grumpy mood. Understandably worried, she could not stop wondering if there was some way she could help him snap out of it.

Finally, she had an idea.

It was a good one.

"A pet," she decided. "The Professor needs a pet."

"If he had to care for someone else, he would have to stop feeling sorry for himself. And as soon as he stops being miserable, he'll start inventing again, and everything will go back to normal."

"That's a great solution. But what kind of pet should it be? And where would I get it from?"

Maud was lucky. She had many good friends in the village, and when she explained the situation to them there were a number of helpful suggestions. Unfortunately, most of them were easy to reject.

No, a snake would not suit the Professor. A boa constrictor might engage him in a wrestling match and give him a good squeeze, but that was not quite the kind of exercise that Maud had in mind.

A bird would not do either. The only way a bird would activate the Professor would be if it were let out of the cage. This would likely cause a mess, so was not a good idea.

She ruled out mice, too small, a horse, too big, and a koala bear, impossible to get hold of.

Maud's friends came up with many clever ideas, but she was beginning to suspect that they were making a joke out of the situation.

She decided to try a different tactic.

"What kind of animal would I prefer, if it was for me?" she asked. "It would have to be cuddly, but not too small. Certainly not too big."

When it came to her, the answer was obvious.

"A dog!"

"Of course," she decided.

No doubt at all. Professor Kompressor was a dog person. A cat would not be right because the Professor needed to be activated. Long strengthening walks, several times a day. That would be just the thing.

Once she had made up her mind, it was a

question of finding a suitable puppy. Again, Maud was lucky. One of her neighbours had a dog that had just had a litter of puppies. They were some odd kind of mongrel which her friend referred to as Jack Daniels, and as he could not keep them all he was happy to give one to Maud. She picked a particularly cheeky looking one. It had a black spot around the right eye and a wiggly tail.

She named him Spot. Her imagination was not at the same level as the Professor's. She was a practical woman.

The next day she brought the puppy over to the Professor's house. On the way, the thing bounced all over the road as if they were on the greatest adventure.

"What infectious happiness," Maud laughed. "Little Spot, you are absolutely going to cheer the Professor up."

When they arrived at the Professor's house, he was sitting in the garden with a cup of tea. Three lumps of sugar and a splash of milk. Doing nothing.

The puppy, on the other hand, was too excited to slow down. He jumped around, all over the place, bumping into things. He ran into the Professor and made him spill his tea. He rolled about in the grass and then scurried off to do some digging in the plant beds.

"Spot!" shouted Maud. "Slow down!"

"Don't..."

"... oh, you little pig!"

The dog was a mess. It was hard to believe that it was possible to get so dirty in such a short time.

"We'd better get you cleaned up," said Maid with a smile, "and then you can say a proper hello to the Professor."

Maud brought the dog into the house, plonked him in the bathtub and showered him clean. She got more or less soaked in the process, but at last the puppy was clean again. Having wrapped him in an old towel, she brought the little parcel back into the garden.

This time she did not make the mistake of letting him run about.

"Hello!" said the Professor. "What a cute little thing."

"What's the name of your new dog, Maud?" he asked.

"Hrrmm", she replied. "It's not my dog. It's yours."

"And his name is Spot."

The Professor looked confused, as if he was about to say something along the lines of "But, I don't have a dog..."

Then he smiled.

"If that's the case, then you're welcome to your new home Spot. I very much hope you'll be happy here."

Spot wagged his tail. There was no doubt that he was expecting to be happy. Wherever he was.

The lively puppy made an immediate impact on the Professor's life. Suddenly there was no time to be bored. In between taking Spot for walks, or playing with him in the garden, there was not much time at all. Of course, there were times when the little dog decided to have a nap on the rug in the hallway. It was a nice place to lie, especially in the afternoon when the sun had warmed up that particular spot. By then the Professor was exhausted, so he usually had a snooze, as well.

Several days passed and things were going

great.

It was a warm afternoon and the Professor was outside throwing a ball, with Spot giving chase. As the dog raced after the ball, he jumped in the air with happy yelps and barks.

"I wonder," thought the Professor. "Wouldn't it be interesting to know what those funny noises mean?"

When they had finished playing, Spot had managed to get himself remarkably messy, so Professor Kompressor had to give him a bath.

That evening he started thinking about an invention. It all came back to him quite naturally, almost as if he had never taken a break.

"I'm going to figure this out," he decided. "I'll invent a translating device so that little Spot can talk to me."

Pleased with the idea, the Professor went to bed.

The following day he did not play with Spot. After the morning walk, he went into the inventing studio to work on the new device.

It was not a very difficult thing to build.

After all, the Professor had already made a voice box for the mechanical maid. He also had the thought control that he had used on the television. All he had to do was combine the two, making sure that the final package was small enough to fit around Spot's neck.

The Professor finished the device in a couple of hours. Then he went looking for Spot to try it out.

He found the dog sleeping in the hallway. Spot looked so peaceful that the Professor did not have the heart to wake him up.

He went into the kitchen to make a cup of tea instead.

The dog slept on, snoring gently.

The Professor waited.

Finally, Spot rolled over. With a big yawn he stretched his legs in all directions at once, turned around and gave the Professor an excited look. He was rested and ready to play.

The Professor grabbed the dog gently, and fixed the collar with the translator around his neck.

At first Spot tried to shrug it off, but when he realized that it was not going to work he gave up.

Professor Kompressor switched on the device.

"Now we'll see," he said to Spot. "It's time to figure out what you're really like."

Spot said nothing. He just stood up and followed the Professor into the garden.

They went for a walk. This time Spot did not chase after butterflies or bees. He did not jump about barking. He seemed quite happy, but he kept quiet.

"Most unusual," thought the Professor. "Not like Spot at all."

On the way back to the house they had to cross a little stream.

Inevitably, Spot plunged in.

Soaking wet he climbed out of the water, shook himself and then decided to roll over in a muddy puddle.

The Professor tried to catch the dog, but he could not quite reach. As he stretched, he slipped in the mud, lost his balance and...

"Splash!"

Happily, Spot jumped onto the wet Professor's lap and licked his face.

"What are you like?" groaned the Professor, glasses askew. "Oh Spot, what are you like?"

"Oink!" said Spot.

CHAPTER 12

The Christmas Delivery

It was the time of year when snow is supposed to cover the countryside like a blanket, making everything look clean and fresh. Icicles dangling from rooftops. Stars sparkling from freezing cold skies.

The rain was bucketing down. It was just a couple of weeks before Christmas and the climate had gone mad. Professor Kompressor had heard about global warming, but he did not use to think much of the idea. This so-called winter was making him reconsider. Then, all of a sudden, the weather changed. From madness to normality in an instant. The temperature dropped and several inches of snow fell. Children had to stay at home because the schools were closed. The Professor had to dig out his warm winter clothes. He also had to dig himself out of the house each morning, just to pick up the post.

The Professor enjoyed winter, but he was

not keen on Christmas. He could not see the point of all the glitzy decorations and the shiny lights. To bring an entire tree inside... for goodness sake! Being a practical man, he obviously did not believe in Father Christmas either. He probably had done when he was a little boy, but he suspected that he had been tricked by his parents. He did not like the thought of that. A man with a white beard, in a factory at the North Pole making toys, and then distributing them one particular night of the year. To all the children in the world. Ridiculous idea. Absolutely ridiculous.

It was Christmas Eve. The Pig-Dog was sleeping on a cushion by the open fire in the sitting room. His legs were twitching as if he were chasing something in his dreams, perhaps a rabbit. He was snoring.

The Professor was sitting in his favourite chair reading a book about the famous inventor Leonardo da Vinci. There were some very interesting sketches in the book, and he was trying to figure out how these machines were supposed to work.

They had had a nice meal. Possibly on the

modest side given the season, but still nice. Now they were settling in for the evening.

It was getting dark outside. It was cold and the skies were clear. A perfect night for stargazing.

Suddenly, they were startled by a loud crash from upstairs.

It sounded as if a large cupboard had fallen over.

Then came a drawn out screech. Something heavy slid down the roof. Loose tiles clattered to the ground.

A second crash. Louder than the first.

Something had fallen off the roof and landed, not very gently, in the back garden.

Spot and the Professor, already on their feet, rushed to see what was going on.

When Professor Kompressor opened the patio doors, he was faced with the most amazing scene.

Chaos reigned in the back garden.

Several large animals with what seemed to be horns on their heads limped around over by the gooseberry bushes.

A large sleigh-like object had crash-landed

in the middle of the lawn.

A round man with a grey beard and a red woolly hat was standing by the sleigh mumbling to himself.

"Oh-oh-oh," he said. "What have we done?"

"Oh, Rudolf, I think we're done for this time..."

The Professor surveyed the scene of the apparent accident. He was too stunned to think clearly. Yet something tickled his memories.

Surely, it could not be. Could it?

Spot had no such reservations. He dashed into the garden, barked happily at the reindeer and jumped up to greet the bearded man.

"Good evening, Spot," cheered the man.

"Who's a good little doggie, then?"

"Have you deserved your Christmas bone? Have you?"

The man scratched Spot behind the left ear. The dog really liked that.

Professor Kompressor finally regained his senses.

"Hmm. Excuse me, but... are you... can't

be..."

The words stumbled out of his mouth.

"Afraid so," said the man. "This old sleigh is going nowhere tonight."

"The children will be so disappointed."

"Dreadful," he added, even though there was no need for it.

Father Christmas turned to Professor Kompressor.

"Do you think?" he started.

"Do you think you could help?"

"Can you fix it?"

It only took the Professor a moment to decide that the answer was a definite no. The sleigh was not going anywhere that night. It was too badly damaged. Besides, the poor reindeer looked dazed and confused. Some of them were limping badly. They needed a rest. The situation could not have been worse.

The Professor's brain was working hard. There had to be a way out of this jam. He could not let the children down. He had to fix this.

But what could he possibly do? The crashed sleigh seemed a non-starter, and they were running out of time.

There was no time for thinking. They needed action. Immediately.

Professor Kompressor was not used to inventing under time pressure. He was not good at dealing with stressful situations. He needed to be in a relaxed frame of mind for the ideas to flow, and he knew that inventions needed to be tested properly. Otherwise they could be quite dangerous. He had learned this the hard way.

There was no time for caution. He had to make quick decisions, and whatever he came up with had to work.

It just had to.

The Professor realized that he would not be able to create something new. He had to recycle.

He had a shedful of discarded inventions. The problem was that they had not worked in the first place. Was there some way that he could cobble something together out of bits and pieces from the shed?

He decided to give it a go.

The obvious starting point was the flying

car. How badly damaged was it? It should have dried out by now, but would the engine work? Could it still fly? And what about the power source? It was night, so solar power was out of the question. Was there a way to replace it? Would batteries work? They only had to last one night. After that it did not matter if they were out of juice.

"It can be done!" said the Professor. "But we'll have to take some risks."

"Risks?" laughed Father Christmas. "Dear Professor. I'm rather familiar with risks. It's not as if it's safe to fly about in a sleigh pulled by reindeer. Bad enough in daylight, but during the night..."

"I think this evening's experience says it all."

They moved over to the shed and dragged the wrecked car into the snowy garden.

It looked a little bit worse for wear, but the damage was mostly cosmetic.

The Professor went into the house, and searched the inventing studio for the extra powerful battery cells that he had been working on. To his great relief, they were fully charged. He picked them up along with some tools and went back outside.

He was concentrating so hard that he did not notice that he was still in his slippers, and it was freezing cold.

Father Christmas watched with a mixture of amazement and amusement as the Professor ripped out parts of the car's engine and threw them in the snow. There was not much he could do. He was not exactly good with mechanical devices. The Professor, however, was excellent at inventing things. And this time the invention would have to be excellent. There were no alternatives.

Professor Kompressor wired up the batteries and jumped into the driver's seat.

When he flicked the switch the car's engine made a noise... and then... nothing.

It did not work.

What was wrong? The Professor tried to think it through, but it was hard to concentrate. There was too much pressure.

He opened the bonnet and glared down at the engine. The construction was a complete mess. He had been tearing bits out and adding new parts, mostly using gaffer tape and bits of string. The end result was a virtual bird's nest of wires, tape and string.

How could he possibly get this to work?

Then it struck him! Reverse double wiring! He had wired the batteries as he would for a normal engine, but this invention was far from normal. Maybe he just had to reverse it?

He dived in, tore off some wires and reattached others.

Back in the driving seat, the Professor tried the switch again. This time the car jumped to life, literally. It lifted off the snow-covered ground and the headlights came on.

Two bright beacons of light lit up the field.

"Get the presents in! Quick!" the Professor called out.

He did not have to say this twice. Father Christmas was already on his way, carrying a massive sack full of presents for children all over the world. He opened the passenger side door and tried to push the sack into the backseat. It was far too big. There was no way that it would fit.

Of course, the sack had been too big for

the sleigh as well. It took a whiff of magic to make room for it.

They were ready to go.

"You'd better drive, Professor," said Father Christmas. "I'll handle the deliveries."

Off they went, zooming over the starlit landscape.

In no time at all, they delivered presents to the houses in the village.

They carried on, making deliveries all over the country.

It was done at incredible speed. They hardly came to a stop at each individual house. Father Christmas was down the chimney and up again in not time at all. Soon the journey turned into a bit of a blur and Professor Kompressor had no idea where they were or where they had been. They pushed on regardless.

They flew over mountain ranges covered with snow, African plains on the edge of the desert, and exotic islands with palm trees.

It was an amazing trip, but they did not have time to stop to enjoy the scenery.

Dawn was approaching. They still had an

entire continent to go. Professor Kompressor pushed the accelerator all the way to the floor. The flying car responded and, even though it seemed impossible, went even faster.

Finally, Father Christmas climbed back into the passenger seat, looked in the back and said, "That's the last one. We did it!"

"Let's go back home."

They returned to Professor Kompressor's house at a more sedate pace, landed by the garden shed and stepped out in the snow. The sun was rising in the east. It was going to be another crispy cold, clear day.

The Professor woke up in the sitting room chair. It was morning. He had had the weirdest dream about helping Father Christmas. Completely bonkers.

He walked over to the window and looked out into the back garden. Fresh snow had fallen. There were certainly no traces of a crashed sleigh.

It was a beautiful morning.

Then he noticed it.

Something was not quite right.

The door to the garden shed had been left

ajar. The flying car, covered by a thin layer of snow, was parked outside.

"Surely not?" thought the Professor.

He went into the kitchen to make some tea. He clearly had not woken up properly yet.

On the kitchen table sat a nicely wrapped present and a note.

"*Dear Professor*," it said.

"*Thank you so much for saving Christmas. I don't know what I would have done without your help. Keep up the good inventing work.*

PS

Maybe I'll see you again next year."

F.C.

ABOUT THE PROFESSOR

Nils Andersson is a real life Professor of Mathematics and a leading authority on Einstein's theory of relativity and extreme astrophysics. At work he worries about black holes, dead stars, white dwarfs and waves of gravity. In his spare time he likes to read. He always did, ever since he was little. As a grown-up he continues to be excited by books for younger readers, great stories that inspire developing minds and make the next generation fall in love with books. A house full of books made him wonder what it would be like to write one of his own. So, with a bit of help from his 7-year old daughter, he did.

Professor Kompressor is a fictional character (certainly not based on the author!) and his adventures are completely made up. Yet, the various episodes draw on ideas from science and the modern world. The aim is to show that you can have a lot of fun with science and technology, especially if you allow for a bit of creative mis-interpretation.

If you enjoyed the Professor's mad inventions, please consider writing an honest review and posting it on the site you bought the book from. It is amazing what a little bit of encouragement can do, especially when it involves sensitive souls like authors.

You can stay up-to-date with the Professor on facebook; simply search for ProfessorKompressorBook.

The author's somewhat related ramblings on science and fiction can be found on www.sciencefunfiction.blogspot.com. Every now and then there is a short inventing story posted there, as well. Worth looking out for.

Enjoy!

9016751R00066

Printed in Great Britain
by Amazon.co.uk, Ltd.,
Marston Gate.